ALL NIGHT LONG

CASE FILES: POCKET-SIZED MURDER MYSTERIES

RACHEL AMPHLETT

ALL NIGHT LONG

ONE

The first twinge of panic set in when Zoe Michaels saw the clock above the collection of vintage license plates tick over to ten.

The Easy Stop diner had been dead for an hour before that, quiet except for the gentle bubble and hiss from the coffee machine where it sat on the counter beside a collection of wooden takeaway forks.

It was drafty in here, the large thin windows facing the parking lot doing little to stop a freezing cold Montana wind from attacking Zoe's shoulders as she peered through the glass. She'd discovered an hour ago that the red and white checked drapes didn't close properly, and that they were merely tacked to the side of each window for show rather than comfort or privacy.

The same could be said for the cracked leather booths that ran the length of the single-story building, save for one that had been half-heartedly reupholstered with a flowery pattern she hadn't seen since her grandmother was alive.

There was condensation on the panes now, the steam from her half-empty coffee mug fogging the glass while the icy air beyond pushed back.

Zoe's stomach rumbled – the food was good here. She had the pancakes with maple syrup two Sundays ago for brunch, and then a burger earlier this afternoon when she and Jake had called in.

It had been warm in here, cozy in fact, when she first entered the diner tonight but the last vestiges of heat had slunk from the building half an hour ago, an hour after she'd turned down the thermostat and switched off the fryers and griddle.

Now the diner only served coffee, and that was only because she was drinking it herself.

She shifted in her seat, her hand peeling from the cheap Formica table with a gentle slurp, and she wrinkled her nose at the tell-tale ketchup stains crossing the chipped and cracked surface.

Another time, another place and she might have smushed a damp cloth across the table, shaken the crumbs onto the floor and then brushed those away with the broom that leaned against a steel shelf laden with cans of beans out in the kitchen.

Not tonight.

Beyond the windows, a pitch-black sky cloaked a desolate highway, the only light coming from the tall neon green and blue sign that matched the one above the entrance to the diner and a pair of spotlights that shone into the oversized parking area for trucks and motor homes.

Not that there were any of those at the moment.

February was too cold for most tourists, and the new year's sales frenzy was a distant memory for a lot of truck drivers. There were mostly only long-distance journeymen now, delivering machine parts and perishable goods and flatpack furniture with no discernible instructions.

She knew that because she'd spotted familiar logos on the sides of the trailers as they'd traveled along the highway in the opposite direction earlier that day.

Thank God for coffee.

Draining her cup, Zoe slid from the booth beside the door and made her way over to the steaming pot.

Wrinkling her nose, she poured another dose.

It was a cheap brand, bought in bulk – she'd seen the cans next to the beans in the kitchen earlier – but it would do.

It would have to do.

She turned back to the door and glared at the empty parking lot.

The waiting was the worst.

Closely followed by the not knowing.

Then the doubt.

Throat dry, she blew across the surface of the hot drink and then sipped.

Whatever happened, it was sure to be a long night ahead and she had to stay alert.

Then headlights appeared in the distance, then

a halo of color, then the silhouette of an enormous truck barreling along the highway towards the diner.

Zoe held her breath, wishing they had simply turned off the neon sign and turned around the sign on the door to 'closed'.

She said it was safer that way, but had lost that argument after being told that people expected the diner to be open all night long.

There was a reputation to maintain, after all.

The truck didn't slow down.

It roared past, a maple leaf emblazoned in LED lights stretching across its radiator grille as it powered north along Route 15.

Zoe smiled when its tail-lights faded into the distance.

She always wanted to visit Canada.

After all, it was only a couple of hours' drive farther north.

So close, and yet…

Another truck emerged from the gloom, traveling from the opposite direction and slowing to a crawl as its indicators flashed.

"Dammit."

The enormous rig was naked, no trailer behind it, and ground its way across the graveled parking lot, the headlights streaming through the windows and blinding her for a moment.

She raised her hand to ward off the glare, then drained her coffee, squared her shoulders and strode around the counter.

As the rig rocked to a standstill facing the

empty highway, Zoe tied an oversized polyester apron around her waist with 'It's easy to stop at the Easy Stop!' printed across the front pocket.

That done, she pulled out her cell phone, reversed the camera and brushed errant streaks of dust from her hair and cheeks, then tried to steady her breathing.

She swallowed, reached out to tweak on the radio next to the till, and took a deep breath as a recent country and western hit filtered through the speakers fitted above the booths.

She could do this.

TWO

11pm

He was tall, at least six feet five, with shoulders that brushed the door frame as he edged his way inside.

An electronic bell rang out at the same time, the noise reverberating from a tiny speaker beside the clock.

Zoe knew she would hear the sound in her sleep for weeks to come.

If she survived.

Dust coated his denim jeans while a tidemark of mud slaked his boots, and she spotted a fine drizzle misting the night air beyond the door before it swung shut behind him.

Removing a battered baseball cap with faded lettering down one side, he raked thick fingers through thinning pale brown hair and eyed her with interest.

"Where's Vince?" his voice rasped.

"He had to go out." Zoe heard the tremor in her voice and forced a smile. "Traveled far?"

"All the way from Calgary." He sank onto one of the steel-framed stools beside the counter, the worn leather cushion farting under his weight. "With any luck, I'll make Spokane before sunrise. What's your name, anyway?"

"Zoe."

"Nice to meet you, Zoe. I'm Henry." He reached out for one of the laminated menus racked against the till and ran a practiced eye down the list. "Tell Bettina I'll have the burger, the works, same as usual."

"Sorry, we're not doing hot food tonight. The fryers are out – so's the griddle. Bettina isn't here, either."

"Fu—" He shook his head, his top lip curling as he snorted in disgust. "I knew I should've pulled into the truck stop ten miles back for food. Only reason I didn't was that there was a line stretching out the door…"

"I'm sorry. We've got coffee though." Zoe watched while he glanced over his shoulder at the truck, his fingers drumming the counter. "I could fix you a sandwich perhaps?"

He turned back and waved his hand as if batting away a bluebottle fly. "Yeah, whatever. Beats turning back, I s'pose."

Scurrying over to the hot plate, Zoe lifted off a fresh pot of steaming coffee and slopped a generous measure into one of the white ceramic mugs lined up on the counter before thrusting it at him. "I'll have to check the kitchen to see what's available."

"If there's any of Vince's bologna, I'll have that."

"Okay."

"Did he leave anything for me? Behind the till there?" He jerked his chin at the two cluttered wooden shelves fixed to the plasterwork beside the serving hatch. "It's usually in one of them small envelope things."

Zoe swept her gaze across the shelves. "There's no envelope here."

"Christ, this just gets better, doesn't it?" Henry waved her away.

She spun on her heel, swiped aside the red and white striped plastic curtain separating the diner from the kitchen and stepped into a stainless steel-lined room that smelled of—

"Don't forget the tomato," he called out in her wake. "And pickle. And use that white bread, none of that healthy stuff with the seeds that get stuck in m' teeth."

Zoe rolled her eyes, huffed her fringe from her eyes and stalked across the non-slip floor towards the refrigerator, the soles of her shoes making a sucking sound with every step.

Walking past the fryers, goosebumps prickled her arms as the remnant warmth reached her, despite them being turned off two hours ago.

A red blinking light flashed on and off above the safety switch, and she bit back a pang of crawling guilt at denying someone a hot meal.

It had to be kept cold in here, otherwise—

The electric flycatcher above the back door emitted a crackling *zap* and she jumped, turning around in time to see a helpless shriveled bug drop between the wire mesh and land amongst the other bodies.

Berating herself, trying to calm her racing heart, she wrenched open the refrigerator door and glared at the contents.

Plastic containers of every shape and size were squashed onto the shelves, some with black marker pen words scrawled across the side naming the contents.

Wrinkling her nose, she rummaged between the cracks, lifting lids and battening down a rising disgust at the number of fat-flecked and greasy combinations left by Vince and Bettina.

No wonder the pair of them wore a few extra chins. Vince in particular had to be two hundred and fifty pounds.

How old was some of this stuff?

Was it safe to eat?

Finding something that resembled the bologna her grandmother used to serve up for Saturday lunches, Zoe sniffed at it tentatively, then pulled the container out and set it on one of the steel counters. She found half a tomato hiding behind a gigantic wedge of parmesan, butter wrapped in grease-proof paper and shoved inside the refrigerator door beside two-day-old full fat milk, and a large jar of pickles on the bottom shelf.

She pulled it out, ignoring the label that suggested it should have been thrown away a month ago, figuring that the truck driver – Henry – had eaten worse in his time on the road, especially if he was a regular here.

Anyway, the sooner he was on his way, the better.

Cutting thick wedges of bread, she made the sandwich and marched back towards the diner.

Henry was stirring sugar into his mug, a small pile of paper sachets discarded on the counter beside him and the spoon clinking against the side of the mug with each turn.

Deep lines raked his forehead, and he rested his chin in his hand while he watched the swirling coffee.

Zoe cleared her throat. "Here you go. Hope it's okay."

She set down the plate on the counter and took a step back as he launched himself at the food.

"At least Vince had the decency not to close," he said, exposing masticated food before taking a second bite. "That wouldn't have gone down well around here."

"Oh? Is he usually busy on a Monday night?"

Henry shrugged, then swallowed and took a swig from the mug before answering. "Not busy, no. But he gets a few regulars like me. As it is, I'll put a call out on the radio to let everyone know there's no hot food tonight. Save them stopping for nothin'."

Zoe's stomach flipped. "Do you have to do that? I mean, it's just…"

He held up his hand. "I know you're doing your best, sugar but this place is a… whaddaya call it?'

"An institution?"

"Yeah. That." He demolished the rest of the sandwich in three mouthfuls, wiped his lips with his sleeve, then belched.

Zoe took a step back as a backwash of meat and pickle wafted over her, scowling as Henry drained his coffee.

"Listen, perhaps don't tell them and I'll try to figure out how the griddle works at least," she said. "There was a power cut earlier and Vince tried everything but…"

"I don't know…"

"But you said there was a line at the other place, right? What if there are others like you, drivers who don't need fuel but just some coffee and something to eat?" She sounded desperate but didn't care.

Because she had to make it look normal.

Business as usual.

Those were his last instructions before he left at nine twenty.

Left her to run the place on her own.

As if she had any idea how.

Henry rose from his seat, and she heard his knees crick in protest.

"Look, you seem a nice girl… Zoe, isn't it?"

She nodded, mute.

"I won't put out a call, but you tell Vince when you see him that people depend on him, all right? He should know that after all this time. It's been, what, eleven years he's been running this place?"

"I'll tell him."

"Good." He winked. "Now I got to go and shake a leg."

Zoe picked up his empty plate as he waddled towards the door for the rest-rooms at the far end of the diner, then stomped into the kitchen and threw the plate into the sink.

It splintered into seven separate pieces and a small cloud of shards before coming to rest against an abandoned pile of utensils, the sound ricocheting off the matching stainless steel splash backs.

Exhaling, she used the hem of the apron to swipe at a trickle of cold sweat that pricked her brow, then straightened her shoulders and checked her watch.

"Come on," she muttered.

The water pipes shook and rattled behind the splash back, a sure sign the toilet in the men's room had been flushed, and she scuttled back to the counter as Henry emerged, wiping his hands down his jeans.

That done, he jabbed his thumb over his shoulder.

"You might want to clean up the men's room if

you're not busy serving hot food. It smells like something died in there."

Zoe mumbled an apology as he chucked a handful of dollar bills on the counter and stalked out the front door, the glass juddering in his wake.

THREE

Midnight

The smell in the kitchen was starting to dissipate with the aid of an ancient electric fan that Zoe found in the back office after Henry left, but the men's room was a whole different matter.

When she pushed open the door, she was assaulted by a stench that was almost prehistoric in nature.

When she flipped on the light switch, a clapped-out ventilation duct rattled and shook itself to life before dying with a polite cough.

Four urinals were lined up against the right-hand wall – the one that backed onto the kitchen – and a single cubicle took up the other. There were pink crumbs of sanitary cakes in two of the urinals. Between those and the cubicle were two chipped and worn ceramic sinks, brown stains slopping from the overflow outlets and limescale clinging to the base of the faucets.

The paper towel dispenser hung empty over one of them.

The truck driver hadn't been kidding, either – it looked like a fight had broken out in here.

"Shit," she said, then ventured over to the cubicle and nudged the door open with the toe of her shoe. "Christ."

She recoiled, covering her nose with her arm and staggering backwards.

Water had sloshed over the floor from the bowl, while a tiny blood splatter smudged across the seat where it congealed quietly. Something off-white clung to the bottom of the pan.

Was that a tooth?

Zoe spun on her heel and hurried through the door, gasping for air.

Beyond the kitchen, she found a narrow cupboard in the back office that contained a motley assortment of cleaning materials – although by the state of the bottles, cleaning wasn't top of Vince and Bettina's priorities.

After blowing recalcitrant dust off a gallon bottle of bleach, she tipped out a spider from a bucket and located a motheaten mop behind a stack of boxes with various import stamps emblazoned across the lids.

Once the bleach was mixed with hot water, she grabbed a spray bottle of multipurpose cleaner and stomped back to the men's room laden with her weaponry.

Cursing under her breath, listening out for the bell warning her of any new customers, Zoe swished the mop back and forth across the laminated floor, her shoes leaving shadowy footprints.

She blinked back tears from the overpowering mix of bleach and pine forest scent while she scrubbed at the toilet bowl, and then wiped down the sinks. That done, she kicked the bright plastic bucket to one side and propped the mop against the tiled wall before leaning against the door frame, exhausted.

When she peered at her shrunken and shriveled fingers, Zoe hissed at the chipped pink acrylic nails and vowed to kill Jake when he returned.

If he returned.

FOUR

1am

Zoe bit back a yawn and watched while fine sleet slashed at the diner's windows, the wind whipping the black and white awning over the door.

Fingers clutched around her phone, she eyed the icon in the top right-hand corner of the screen and bit her lip.

How long did twenty per cent battery last?

Her thumb hovered over the phone icon for a split second, and then she pressed it.

Three rings, four, then—

"This is Jake. I can't take your call right now. You know what to do."

Beep.

"Where the hell are you?' she spat. 'It's been nearly four hours. If you've—"

She hung up, the rest of her tumbling thoughts unsaid.

Maybe if she spoke it out loud, it would be true, and she didn't want that.

Couldn't have that.

He had to be coming back for her, had to be.

He'd promised.

Eighteen per cent.

"Shit."

Tucking the phone in her jeans pocket, she frowned and then reached out to turn down the radio as another sound filtered through the thin windows.

Sirens.

Coming closer.

Suddenly her heart tried to burst from her chest like one of those monsters in that sci-fi movie she'd streamed the other month.

Her throat constricted, bile threatening as the sirens grew louder, louder, and then—

Then a police cruiser zipped past, its red and blue lights flaring through the sleet, the driver ignoring the speed limit as the vehicle powered towards Spokane.

It was gone in seconds, its rear lights flashing once before the car crested the subtle rise in the camber a quarter of a mile away and disappeared.

Zoe turned and wrenched open the soft drinks cabinet, her fingers sliding down the condensation on the steel handle before she plucked out a can and popped the lid.

She drained half, then slammed the door shut, panting.

Pushing apart the plastic curtain, she peered into the kitchen and wondered whether it was worth trying the car once more.

After all, maybe Jake had just flooded the engine turning the key over and over again.

Maybe the cooling air had been enough to release whatever mechanism had overheated or…

"Fuck!"

The curtain slapped back into place and Zoe brought a shaking fist to her mouth.

Jake had the keys.

FIVE

2am

Twelve per cent.

Zoe forced her gaze away from the phone propped against the abandoned laptop computer and turned her attention to the desk drawers.

Surely Vince kept a spare pair of car keys somewhere?

He and Bettina had a small clapboard house a few hundred yards back from the diner, less than a minute's walk across the frozen stony earth.

It was a desolate place that had chilled her skin as soon as she'd stepped over the threshold.

She'd searched through the kitchen, and then explored the box-like bedroom at the back of the house with its quilted counterpane and threadbare carpeted floors but returned to the diner empty-handed.

Vince's old Ford pickup shielded Jake's twenty-year-old sedan from the highway, and as she glanced through the window above the desk, she saw it had also shielded it from the worst of the thickening sleet. An arc of light blue paint still showed through the sprinkles whereas the pickup truck now wore a soft white hat almost half an inch deep.

If Jake didn't get back here soon…

She froze at the sound of a rumbling engine, the floor vibrating under her feet, then slammed the desk doors shut and tightened Bettina's enormous apron around her waist.

Snatching up the phone, she dialed him again as she made her way back towards the diner, adrenaline spiking her heart rate once more.

"Jake, it's been five hours. Where the hell are you?" she said, hating the desperation in her voice. "Babe – call me, okay?"

When she reached the counter, she gasped.

It was now snowing heavily, thick flakes spinning in the wind and striking the windows. The stony parking area out front was already covered, and as she watched the truck glide to a standstill with a familiar online store logo emblazoned like a sardonic smile down the side of its trailer, her mouth dried.

What if Jake had had an accident?

What if he never came back?

"He's okay," she murmured. "He's got to be okay."

The driver's door opened, and a figure bounced

to the ground, swaddled within a thick padded coat.

Zoe turned away, taking a few seconds to close her eyes and focus before switching the coffee pots around to start a fresh batch.

By the time he opened the door, the rich aroma of Arabica beans filled the room and she blew on her fingers to warm them.

At least he wouldn't want to stay long.

"Evening," she managed, turning to face him.

"Boy, am I glad you're open." He ruffled open his coat, sending a spray of ice crystals and rain across the tiled floor and exposing a collared shirt with the same logo as the one on the trailer across the left pocket. "I didn't know if you would be in this."

Melting snow dripped from his forehead, and he slicked back wet hair with a paw of a hand.

"Hot drinks only, I'm afraid but I can fix you a sandwich to go with it if you like?"

"Vince's bologna sandwich?" He grinned and patted his substantial gut. "That'll do me. The ex-wife reckoned I eat too much junk anyway."

Zoe matched his smile.

Maybe it would be okay after all.

SIX

3am

Carl was his name.

Fifty-six, lived in Drummond, happily divorced.

"I've got a daughter. About the same age as you, I reckon. She's a schoolteacher in Missoula." Carl's eyes softened, and after dabbing at his phone screen a couple of times, he turned it around to face her. "That's her, with her partner Diane."

"That's nice." Zoe turned away, wiping the cloth across the counter.

"Yeah. They've got two dogs, too. Shiatzus. Tiny things."

She heard the note of disdain in his voice and glanced up. "Don't you like dogs?"

"I do, but they're not exactly proper dogs, are they?" He placed his phone on the counter and took another bite from his sandwich, chewing loudly. "I mean, it's not like they're a Great Dane or something like that. A Rottweiler, for instance. I've seen rats bigger than these two."

Zoe laughed, despite everything.

"So how come Vince and Bettina aren't around tonight?"

She shrugged, her smile fading. "They had to go out at short notice."

Carl frowned. "How long have you been here?"

"Started at eight."

Six fucking hours ago.

"This your first shift?"

"Yeah." She pouted. "Does it show?"

"You're doing just fine. Shame the fryers and griddle are out though. I mean, don't get me wrong, the coffee's great but it's freezing outside." He spun on the stool to look at the parking lot. "At least it's a dead night for you though."

"True." She waited until he turned back to his food. "I don't suppose you've got a phone charger I could borrow while you're having that?"

His bottom lip puckered before he shook his head. "Sorry, hon. I plug mine into a USB thingy in the truck while I'm driving. I don't use a charger. I probably would if I had to stay more than two nights anywhere but I got out of the real long haul game three years back. Say, does that TV work?"

Zoe's gaze traveled to the beat-up flat screen

on the bracket above the booth at the far end. "I don't know. I haven't tried it."

"The clicker thing's behind you. Wouldn't mind seeing the weather report." Carl jerked his head towards the window. "Hopefully, that's not going to get any worse before I reach Ellensburg."

"I think the batteries are dead." She picked up the remote and turned it in her hands.

Truth be told, she didn't want to switch on the TV.

Didn't want to see the weather report.

Certainly didn't want to see the news.

"Ah, give it a go. Otherwise, there'll be a manual button underneath the screen. I can always try that."

Fuck it.

Zoe aimed the remote at the screen, which flashed to life in a split second, sound roaring through the diner.

"Woah." Carl reared back at the sensory overload, then turned to her as she thumbed the controls and the reportage returned to a normal level. "Guess Vince and Bettina must've been blasting out the music channels earlier today, eh?"

"Someone must've been." She managed a smile, put down the remote with a trembling hand and eyed the TV while a forecaster started to wave his hand over an isobar graphic. "There's your weather report."

They watched in silence while the forecaster assured viewers that the snowstorm would pass quickly with only minimal disruption, then handed back to the studio presenters.

A good-looking man in his late thirties faced the camera, his face caked with artificial tan and his suit pressed within an inch of its life as his features took on a somber expression.

"Earlier today, a brazen robbery at a pawnshop in Missoula resulted in shots being fired and the suspects making off with the weekend's takings. Megan Browning is at the scene now, and brings us this update, starting with newly released footage from a bystander."

The picture cut from the studio to what was evidently a video captured on a cell phone.

Zoe held her breath while the shaky footage tracked across a street and along a strip mall following two figures in hoodies running towards the end of the block. A pistol was clearly visible in the hand of the taller of the two and there was a black canvas backpack over the shoulder of the other – and then they disappeared down an alleyway.

The report cut from the amateur video to a dark snow-blustered street with two patrol cars parked in front of crime scene tape that flapped against the wind, the emergency lights flaring through the snowfall before the camera panned to a female reporter huddled within a gray parka and clasping a microphone in gloved hands.

"The suspects were caught on camera crossing an intersection before eluding officers sent to the scene, and remain at large," she said. "Police are asking anyone with information regarding the robbery or who might recognize the two thieves to contact them using the phone number now on your screens…"

The presenter in the studio leaned towards the camera, his eyes eager. "Megan, were there any fatalities during the robbery?"

"No-one was injured during this brazen theft," Megan responded, with a note of disappointment in her smiley voice. "The police commissioner has promised a full update in due course."

'That was Megan Browning, reporting from…'

Zoe aimed the remote and hit the 'off' button before sliding it across the counter.

It hit the side of the till with a clang.

Carl turned to her, wide-eyed. "Wow. Guess they'll have a hard time finding them in this weather, too."

"I guess." She shivered, then eyed his empty cup. "D'you want another?"

"No, best be going. I know the weather report said this was easing off, but there are plenty of idiots out there who don't know how to drive in snow – or ice. Back in a sec."

He wandered off to the men's room – *clean* men's room, she reminded herself – leaving behind a waft of stale cigarette smoke and hours-old deodorant.

She hoped he reached Ellensburg.

She'd enjoyed talking with him, almost as if it were a normal thing to do.

In the circumstances.

Minutes later, the door swung open and Carl returned, tucking his cotton shirt into his jeans before shrugging on the thick padded coat.

"Thanks for stopping by," Zoe said.

"You stay safe, you hear? And lock the door after I'm gone." He dropped a couple of dollars into the glass tip jar beside the till before pointing at the blank TV screen. "You never know who's out on these roads. You should take more care. At least until Vince gets back."

"I will, thanks."

SEVEN

4am

Zoe jerked awake, her eyes blinking open and her neck stiff from where she'd fallen asleep at the booth in the corner.

A sickness clawed her stomach as she ran her gaze over the empty diner while she rubbed at her arms, cursing under her breath.

Sliding across the seat, she groaned as pins and needles stabbed at her legs before stumbling towards the counter.

There were no missed calls on her phone, no indication that anyone had walked in during those lost twenty minutes and no tell-tale markings in the light dusting of snow covering the parking lot.

"Stupid," she muttered, berating herself.

She couldn't afford to make a mistake.

Not now.

Reaching across the counter, she pulled out the notes from the tip jar, the irony of Carl adding a couple of dollars not lost on her given that she'd already emptied the contents into her purse seven hours ago for good measure.

Thirty bucks in total.

Yesterday, she would have considered it a small fortune.

Today…

Eight per cent.

Tearing her eyes away from the phone screen, she peered out the windows to the desolate highway beyond the parking lot, willing him to return.

Six hours ago, his lanky form had been swallowed up by a fine swirling mist as he crossed the highway to wait for salvation. It appeared twenty minutes later in the form of a languid driver in a truck with Wyoming license plates who paused for the five seconds it took for Jake to swing himself up into the cab, and then he was gone.

An angry hiss reached her, and she eyed the empty coffee pots that now choked out smoke and fumes and not much else.

She couldn't drink anymore.

The caffeine wasn't working to keep her awake anyway, and she rubbed at tired eyes, biting back a yawn.

"No more sitting down, Michaels."

Blinking once more, Zoe squinted through the glass in the door as lights appeared on the darkened horizon, gradually working their way closer.

Whoever it was, they were following the speed limit, steadily drawing nearer to the diner with every passing second.

It wasn't a truck, that much was certain.

The headlights were too low down, too close together.

She strained her ears but could hear no sirens, and no flashing red and blue lights erupted from the roof of the vehicle.

Reaching around her waist, Zoe picked at the apron strings with trembling fingers, pulling at the bow before wrenching the damn thing over her head and squishing it up in her hands.

She threw it on the counter and then made her way to the door as the vehicle swung into the diner's parking area.

It didn't stop.

Instead, it barreled past the windows, the engine a dull roar and a flash of paintwork catching her eye before it disappeared around the corner of the building.

Holding her breath, Zoe hugged her thick sweater and waited, her ankle boots frozen to the cheap linoleum tiles.

Seconds passed.

Two minutes.

Then a figure appeared, hurrying through the fine rain that was chasing away the last of the snow before jogging up the three steps to the door and wrenching it open.

"Jake!" She levitated into his arms in one leap, wrapping her legs around his back and clinging on while she buried her nose in his neck. "What the hell took you so long?"

"It's okay, it's okay Zo. I'm here now." He ran his hands down her back, then eased her to the ground and cupped her face between his fingers, kissing her nose. "I'm here."

"I tried calling you. Why didn't you answer your phone?"

"It went dead. I forgot to put it on charge this morning before we left." He unzipped his coat and held up his phone before his eyes narrowed and he swept his gaze around the diner. "Any trouble?"

"Two customers, that's all." She turned and led the way past the counter and through the plastic curtain.

"How'd you get on with the safe?"

"He lied about the combination."

"Bastard." Jake wandered across the kitchen floor to where Vince's bloodied and battered body lay slumped at the base of the fryers.

Thick viscous blood was mixed with drool at the corner of the man's mouth, dried and frozen in time. His dead eyes were open wide in fear and pain, his hair still damp in places and hanging lankly across his forehead.

Jake shook his head and sighed. "I really thought he was telling the truth after all that."

"It's okay. I managed to drill the lock out."

Zoe took Jake by the arm and steered him towards the back office, careful to step over

Bettina who sprawled face-down beside the stainless steel sinks below the window, the back of her skull blasted apart by a 9mm round.

The sound had reverberated through the diner, despite Jake jacking up the volume on the TV before dragging Vince through to the men's room to demonstrate the Midwest interpretation of waterboarding.

She paused at the threshold while Jake crossed to the desk, his footsteps tentative.

On the floor beside a framed reproduction print of a pair of racehorses was an array of power tools, including a drill and a crowbar she'd found in a shed off to the side of Vince and Bettina's ramshackle home.

"It took me half an hour," she said, jerking her chin towards the gaping hole in the wall, "but it was worth it."

The safe was empty, its contents now divided amongst the three black canvas bags that sat on the floor at her feet, bundles of cash stacked neatly together in tens and twenties.

All worn, all well-thumbed, all non-traceable.

Jake's eyes widened as he stared at the haul, and he gave an audible swallow. "This is it, babe. Our life savings. Lucky no-one else figured out what Vince was really up to here."

Zoe grinned, affecting Bettina's lisp. "Would you like amphetamines with your coffee? One shot or two?"

"Laugh all you want, but they were here for

eleven years." Jake's voice was full of wonder. "Imagine how much money they were making."

"Then why live in a shithole like this?" Zoe shivered. "You should see the house – it's even worse."

"All a front, I'll bet." Jake crouched by the larger of the three bags and started shoveling in the bundles of notes that were attempting to escape. "They've probably got another place miles away from here, tucked away nice and safe. Maybe in that forest we drove through, by the lake or something like that. Here, help me with these."

She joined him, shoveling the cash from the safe into the nearest black canvas bag. "I told you that car of your brother's was a shit heap."

"It got us this far, didn't it? Besides, if we hadn't broken down, we'd have never found out what Vince was up to." He shrugged. "Sliding doors, babe. It is what it is."

Zipping up the second of the three black canvas bags, Zoe glanced over her shoulder. "What about the stuff from the pawnshop?"

He looked at the pile of valuables scattered across the floor that glittered under the strip lighting. "Just the cash. Leave everything else. And hurry."

"Hurry, says the man who's been MIA for the past six hours."

"I'm serious." Jake reached out and grabbed her wrist. "We picked a fight with the wrong people here, Zo. We can't stay here any longer. It's all over the airwaves."

"That fucking truck driver," she hissed. "He promised he wouldn't tell everyone the diner wasn't serving food."

"Well, he lied. I overheard someone talking about it at the truck stop ten miles back." Jake straightened and swung the thicker of the bags over his shoulder, his knees almost buckling under the weight. "There were two heavies wandering around asking questions, and they won't be far behind. I overheard one of them mention back-up."

"He asked about an envelope. The truck driver, Henry. He was expecting Vince to hand something over."

"Amphetamines, or cocaine." He jerked his head towards the refrigerators nearest the office, the ones that weren't plugged in and that now stood with their doors open, the contents spilling across the floor. "Take your pick, there's enough in those to supply half of Idaho and Washington, never mind the locals."

Zoe picked up the other two bags and hefted them towards the back door. "Any trouble getting the car?"

"No. Come on."

He ripped open the back door, and she took a step back as a gust of wind slapped her face.

"Wait, I need my coat."

"Go. I'll put these in the trunk."

She raced through to the diner, snatched up her parka and ran back, half-expecting to see another car pulling off the road, her heart smashing against her ribcage.

Jake was throwing the last bag in the trunk when she reached the back door, and she slowed to a walk as she approached the car, eyeing the bright red paintwork.

"It's not exactly subtle, is it?"

"It's all I could find at short notice. Besides, I had to hitch-hike thirty miles to find this. It's the middle of the night and we're in the middle of nowhere, Zo. Fucking nowhere."

She folded her arms across her chest. "Ours would've been okay if you hadn't insisted on taking the forest route."

"We had to, otherwise the cops would've picked us up on the 90." He flashed her a smile, the one that sent butterflies chasing around her stomach, then tapped the license plate with the toe of his boot. "Besides, I changed these at the truck stop. Some woman with a silver sedan is none the wiser, and she's currently traveling back to Bozeman."

Zoe exhaled. "If that bitch hadn't thrown the pickup keys out the kitchen door, we could've taken that and been miles away by now."

"Did you find them?"

She threw her arms out sideways. "Are you kidding me? In this weather?"

"I only wondered.' He held up his hands. 'Doesn't matter now anyway. Get in."

Weary, her last reserves of energy spurring her on at the thought of Vince's paymasters catching up with them before they escaped, Zoe sank into the passenger seat and leaned forward to turn up the heater.

The leather seat enveloped her shoulders, cradling her tired limbs, and she smiled as Jake twisted the key in the ignition.

"Love you, Jake."

He reached over for her hand, pressing her fingers to his lips. "Love you too, Zo. Now let's go."

Careful not to let the powerful engine force the sports car into a skid as they left the diner's parking lot and edged onto the highway, he settled his hands on the steering wheel and adjusted the rear-view mirror.

"Right, babe – no stopping until we get north on the 31. I've got someone on standby to cut the power before we reach the border so we can get as close as we can in darkness, then we'll dump this thing and walk over, away from the road."

Zoe nodded in reply, fastened her seat belt, and began to sing under her breath as Jake planted his foot on the accelerator.

"O, Canada…"

THE END

ABOUT THE AUTHOR

Rachel Amphlett is a USA Today bestselling author of crime fiction and spy thrillers, many of which have been translated worldwide.

Her novels are available in eBook, print, and audiobook formats from libraries and retailers as well as her website shop.

A keen traveller, Rachel has both Australian and British citizenship.

Find out more about Rachel's books at: www.rachelamphlett.com.

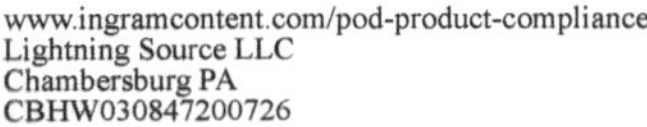